The King of Kites

of Kites

Judith Heneghan
and Laure Fournier

Evans

Anil knew about kites.

He knew how to make them out of paper, sticks and glue. He knew how to fly them in the sky above the village.

The other children brought him their
broken kites to mend.

Anil was the King of Kites.

Anil's mother knew how to sew.
She knew how to cut cloth and stitch seams. She knew how to work beautiful patterns in bright silk.

The other women brought her their old clothes to mend.

She was the Queen of Needles.

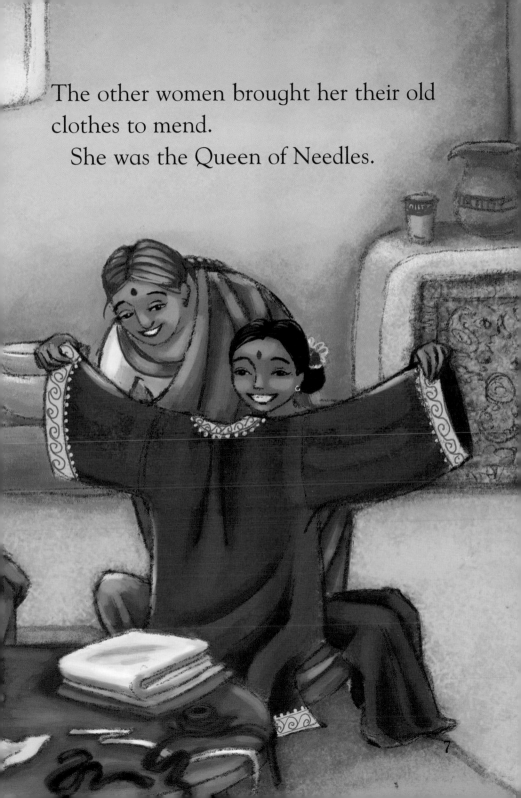

Every morning, Anil and his
mother sat down in a corner of
the yard.

Anil's mother had
everything she needed:
folds of fabric, reels of
thread and a pot of shiny
new pins.

She set to work and
soon her needle flew.

9

Anil, too, had everything he needed:
sheets of paper, spools of string and a
pot of good strong glue. He set to work
and soon his fingers flew.

Then, one day, Anil heard about a
wedding in the village.

"I shall make twelve kites and fly
them all at once in honour of the bride,"
said Anil to his friends. "I shall cover
them with sequins and give them tails
of bright ribbon."

He sat down in the shade and set
to work.

But Anil's mother was not pleased.

"I shall have extra shirts and saris to sew for the wedding!" she cried. "You don't have time for kites, Anil! I need your help, and I need your sequins and your ribbon!"

It was true. The whole village wanted
new clothes for the wedding.

Anil's mother sat down in the
shade and set to work.

All day long she cut and sewed
and stitched.

"I need more cloth!" she cried, and
Anil ran straight to the market.
"I need more thread!" she cried,
and back he went again.

"Anil!" called his friends. "Where are the twelve new kites for the wedding?"

Anil did not answer. His mother had cut up his kite paper for her sari patterns. She had used his string when she ran out of thread.

21

By nightfall all the new clothes were ready. But Anil felt sad. How could he go to the wedding without the kites?

Anil's friends saw that he was sad. They had not forgotten his promise to fly kites at the wedding.

When Anil woke up the next morning, twelve kites lay on the ground outside his house – the kites he had made for his friends long ago!

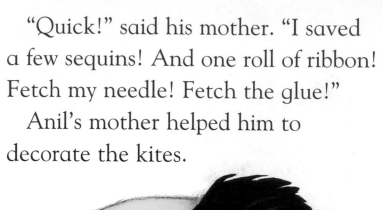

"Quick!" said his mother. "I saved
a few sequins! And one roll of ribbon!
Fetch my needle! Fetch the glue!"
Anil's mother helped him to
decorate the kites.

At the wedding, everyone praised Anil's mother for her stitching.

She was the Queen of Needles.

And everyone admired Anil's twelve beautiful kites flying high in the sky.

28

Anil thanked his friends for giving him their kites. They laughed and lifted him up onto their shoulders.

"You made them for us, Anil!" they shouted. "You are the King of Kites!"

Why not try reading another **Spirals** book?

Megan's Tick Tock Rocket by Andrew Fusek Peters, Polly Peters
HB: 978 0237 53348 0 PB: 978 0237 53342 7

Growl! by Vivian French
HB: 978 0237 53351 0 PB: 978 0237 53345 8

John and the River Monster by Paul Harrison
HB: 978 0237 53350 2 PB: 978 0237 53344 1

Froggy Went a Hopping by Alan Durant
HB: 978 0237 53352 9 PB: 978 0237 53346 5

Amy's Slippers by Mary Chapman
HB: 978 0237 53353 3 PB: 978 0237 53347 2

The Flamingo Who Forgot by Alan Durant
HB: 978 0237 53349 6 PB: 978 0237 53343 4

Glub! by Penny Little
HB: 978 0237 53462 2 PB: 978 0237 53461 5

The Grumpy Queen by Valerie Wilding
HB: 978 0237 53460 8 PB: 978 0237 53459 2

Happy by Mara Bergman
HB: 978 0237 53532 2 PB: 978 0237 53536 0

Sink or Swim by Dereen Taylor
HB: 978 0237 53531 5 PB: 978 0237 53535 3

Sophie's Timepiece by Mary Chapman
HB: 978 0237 53530 8 PB: 978 0237 53534 6

The Perfect Prince by Paul Harrison
HB: 978 0237 53533 9 PB: 978 0237 53537 7

Tuva by Mick Gowar
HB: 978 0237 53879 8 PB: 978 0237 53885 9

Wait a Minute, Ruby! by Mary Chapman
HB: 978 0237 53882 8 PB: 978 0237 53888 0

George and the Dragonfly by Andy Blackford
HB: 978 0237 53878 1 PB: 978 0237 53884 2

Monster in the Garden by Anne Rooney
HB: 978 0237 53883 5 PB: 978 0237 53889 7

Just Custard by Joe Hackett
HB: 978 0237 53881 1 PB: 978 0237 53887 3

The King of Kites by Judith Heneghan
HB: 978 0237 53880 4 PB: 978 0237 53886 6